BO
AMERICA'S
COMMANDER IN LEASH™

Naren Aryal
Illustrated by **Danny Moore**

When I first arrived at the White House, I didn't know what to expect. Sure, I knew that the mansion located at 1600 Pennsylvania Avenue in Washington, D.C. was the home of President Barack Obama and his lovely family. I also knew that being part of the First Family made me the envy of dogs all around the world. What dog wouldn't want to be the "First Dog," the "First Pet," or the "Commander in Leash?"

Bo Obama, a Portuguese water dog, arrived at the White House in 2009. Bo was a gift to the Obama family from Senator Edward Kennedy and his wife, Victoria.

I'm a Portuguese water dog. For centuries, my ancestors have been helping fishermen with their duties. We're well-known for being intelligent, excellent swimmers, and of course, great companions. While I can't go fishing here, the White House is still a great place for a dog. There are lush, green grounds to explore, beautiful gardens and flower beds, long hallways to roam, and history abounds at every turn. There are so many exciting things to see and enjoy here. Let me tell you more about my life at the White House!

The White House was built between 1792 and 1800 and has been the residence of every President, with the exception of George Washington.

Barack Obama became the 44th President of the United States of America on January 20, 2009.

Because President Obama's office is in the shape of an oval, it's known as the "Oval Office." Very important meetings are held in this room. I know to be super quiet here. President Obama has invited me into the Oval Office to meet world leaders, join staff meetings, and sometimes just to keep him company while he works. You know what they say about a dog being man's best friend, right?

One day, I was feeling a little mischievous and decided to swipe the Presidential letter opener from the President's desk. Always a good sport, President Obama played along with my antics and chased me around the room, calling "Give that back, Bo!" I was afraid that I might end up in the Presidential doghouse after that stunt!

When President Obama and his family moved into the White House they added a swing set for the First Kids on the South Lawn. We spend a lot of time playing on the swing set. One day, while swinging high in the air, I decided to try a new trick. I hopped off my swing and went flying through the air. Wow, that was cool! The First Kids yelled, "You're a flying dog, Bo!" My favorite part of the playground is the secret clubhouse atop the equipment. We hold members-only meetings up there and make secret plans for fun things to do all around the White House.

In 1913, First Lady Ellen Wilson replaced Edith Roosevelt's colonial garden with the Rose Garden.

After playing on the swing set, I sometimes venture over to the Rose Garden, where there's always something interesting happening. Not too long ago, a little league baseball team joined the President for a ceremony to celebrate their championship season. White House guests often bring the President souvenirs, but this time, the team brought me a jersey…with my name on it! The team cheered, "Way to go, Bo!"

Over fifty varieties of fruits and vegetables are grown in the White House organic garden.

Every March, the weather begins to warm and signs of spring can be found all around the White House. Mrs. Obama invites local school children to help her plant fruits and vegetables in the new organic garden. The White House kitchen uses food from the organic garden in their preparation of gourmet meals.

Since I love to eat healthy fruits and vegetables, I was happy to learn about the new garden. However, I wasn't too happy when I heard about the new White House beehive. One day, I got a little too close and found myself surrounded by a swarm of buzzing bees. Yikes!

The Obama family began a tradition of dyeing the White House fountains green on St. Patrick's Day.

On St. Patrick's Day, I had the honor of dumping green dye into the White House fountains. I was also in charge of making sure that everyone was wearing green. I spotted a very serious-looking secret service agent that wasn't wearing even a bit of green. With a little nip at his backside, I reminded him that it was St. Patrick's Day. "Ouch, Bo!" he laughed.

The Easter egg roll is always a crowd favorite. At this event, kids meet characters, enjoy arts and crafts, listen to book readings and concerts, and participate in the famous egg roll. I made everyone laugh by rolling my egg with my nose! Children cheered, "Go, Bo, go!"

The first Easter egg roll was organized by Dolly Madison, the wife of President James Madison, in 1814. Until 1877, the event was held on the grounds of the United States Capitol.

After all of that exercise, I was ready to relax to some good music. My favorite band happened to be performing on a nearby stage, but instead of relaxing, I jumped on stage and joined the fun. With so many screaming fans, I could hardly hear myself think! I jammed with the group, delighting the fans gathered on the South Lawn. "Rock on, Bo!" said the band's lead singer.

Easter wouldn't be complete without visiting the Easter Bunny. I posed for a picture with the guest of honor before my fluffy, floppy-eared friend hopped along to see more children.

On Independence Day, there's no better place to be than Washington, D.C. Visitors come to the Nation's Capital from all over the world to experience patriotic parades, concerts, and fireworks.

The Fourth of July barbecue at the White House is much like celebrations held in backyards and parks all over our great country. One year, President Obama appointed me the Fourth of July grill master. I was responsible for flipping burgers and cooking hot dogs. After serving up a plate of goodies to Vice President Biden, he said, "Good grilling, Bo!"

Every Fourth of July, Americans celebrate the adoption of the Declaration of Independence.

The National Mall in Washington, D.C. is the site of one of the largest annual fireworks displays on Independence Day.

After a full day of fun, darkness settled in and the much-anticipated fireworks show began. Brilliant fireworks exploded over the National Mall, and with every colorful burst, "ooohs" and "ahhs" could be heard all around. I sure felt proud to be an American on this day!

The White House is a great place to get sporty. Everyone knows that President Obama loves to play basketball. One day, he invited me to join him and two friends for a friendly game of hoops. I laced up my high-tops and got ready for some action. President Obama dazzled everyone with his amazing basketball skills. After swishing yet another three-pointer, his teammate cheered, "Nice shot, Mr. President!"

President Obama started playing basketball as a child, and he has continued playing throughout his life, even after being elected President.

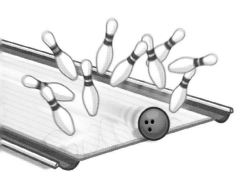

When it comes to bowling, however, there's no question that the Commander in Leash is better than the Commander in Chief! First up was President Obama. He promptly rolled his ball right into the gutter, missing every single pin. I tried not to laugh, but it was very funny! On my turn, I knocked all the pins down! Always a good sport, President Obama congratulated me and said, "Nice strike, Bo!"

The United States Marine Corps helicopter that transports the President is known as "Marine One."

One hot summer day, President Obama told us that we'd be heading to a place called Camp David for the weekend. I discovered that Camp David was in Maryland, not too far from Washington, D.C., and we'd be getting there aboard the Presidential helicopter. How exciting! With a salute from a brave American serviceman, we boarded the aircraft.

As we lifted high into the air, I stuck my head out of the helicopter's window and enjoyed spectacular views of the amazing monuments below. I also enjoyed the cool breeze as it blew through my fur.

CAMP DAVID

Camp David has been used as a Presidential retreat since 1942.

At Camp David, we took a long hike through the woods and explored the natural surroundings. It was great exercise, but afterward, I was ready to cool off at the swimming pool. I dove in with a huge splash, getting everybody wet. "Nice cannonball, Bo!" the First Family hollered.

A turkey has been presented to every President since 1947, but it was President George H.W. Bush that began officially pardoning a Thanksgiving turkey in 1989.

When the weather cools and the leaves turn beautiful fall shades, it's time to start thinking about Thanksgiving at the White House. A few days before the holiday, the President was presented a big, plump turkey. Keeping in line with tradition, the bird was spared by a Presidential pardon. Overcome with happiness, the turkey gobbled, "Thank you, Mr. President, thank you!"

The busiest place during this holiday is the White House kitchen. The chefs work frantically to prepare a traditional meal, complete with all the fixings.

One year, I snuck into the kitchen hoping to sample the pumpkin pie. Unfortunately, the pie fell off the table…and right on my head! A chef laughed and said, "Bon appétit, Bo!"

When the time finally came to enjoy the Thanksgiving feast, everyone was happy to be in the company of friends and family. As Americans, we have so much to be thankful for.

Every year, the White House Christmas tree is delivered aboard a horse-drawn carriage. My first holiday season at the White House, I raced to greet the horses as they made the special delivery. In a tired voice, the horses neighed, "Hello, Bo! Happy Holidays!"

But that's not the only symbol of the season around here. The enormous National Christmas Tree and National Hanukkah Menorah are located on The Ellipse, which is very close to the White House. One year, the President and First Lady invited me to participate in the grand illumination ceremony for both the tree and the menorah!

The National Christmas Tree first appeared in 1923 and the National Hanukkah Menorah was first lit in 1979.

Of course, the holidays wouldn't be complete without a visit to Santa Claus.
I hopped on Santa's lap and handed him my lengthy wish list. Before discussing
all the items on my list, Santa asked, "Have you been a good dog this year, Bo?"

The Alligator
Belonged to John Quincy Adams

Nanny the Goat
Belonged to Abraham Lincoln

Macaroni the Pony
Belonged to John F. Kennedy

I hope you've enjoyed learning all about my life at the White House.
As you can see, it's a lot of fun being a part of the First Family. At the end
of each day, I'm worn out from all the activities and I'm ready for some rest.

PETE the Bull Terrier
Belonged to Theodore Roosevelt

Rex the King Charles Spaniel
Belonged to Ronald Reagan

Socks the Cat
Belonged to Bill Clinton

As I drift off to sleep, I sometimes dream about all the First Pets that have preceded me, and I feel honored to be a part of such a long and distinguished group. But most of all, I feel proud to have the opportunity to serve as America's Commander in Leash!

To my little animal-lover and Bo's number one fan, Maya Katherine; to my
little reader and the inspiration for Mascot Books, Annapurna Elizabeth;
to my wife, Aimee; and to the Obama family.

—Naren Aryal

This one goes out to my Mom and Pops for having me and handing
me a pencil and paper; to the rest of my family for being the coolest;
and to the readers for being the reason we do this!

—Danny Moore

Special thanks to:

Brad Vinson, Josh Patrick, Sue Page, Kim Kuykendall, and Shani Seidel

Contact Bo at bo@mascotbooks.com

www.mascotbooks.com

For more information, please contact Mascot Books,
P.O. Box 220157, Chantilly, VA 20153-0157

ISBN: 1-934878-70-7

Printed in the United States

BO
AMERICA'S
COMMANDER IN LEASH™

Bo is one busy puppy!

More great adventures starring Bo coming soon!

Email bo@mascotbooks.com to receive notification about new titles.

MASCOT BOOKS®

www.mascotbooks.com

ELEMENTARY SCHOOL PROGRAM

Promote reading. Build spirit. Raise money.™

Mascot Books® is creating customized children's books for public and private elementary schools all across America. Containing school-specific story lines and illustrations, our books are beloved by principals, librarians, teachers, parents, and of course, by young readers.

Our books feature your mascot taking a tour of your school, while highlighting all the things and events that make your school community such a special place.

The Mascot Books Elementary School Program is an innovative way to promote reading and build spirit, while offering a fresh, new marketing or fundraising opportunity.

Starting Is As Easy As 1-2-3!

1 You tell us all about your school community. What makes your school unique? What are your well-known traditions? Why do parents and students love your school?

2 With the information you share with us, Mascot Books creates a one-of-a-kind hardcover children's book featuring your school and your mascot.

3 Your book is delivered!